CW01066645

THE DEMON PIANO

TRANSWORLD PUBLISHERS LTD
61–63 Uxbridge Road, London W5 5SA

TRANSWORLD PUBLISHERS (AUSTRALIA) PTY LTD
15-23 Helles Avenue, Moorebank, NSW 2170

TRANSWORLD PUBLISHERS (NZ) LTD
Cnr Moselle and Waipareira Aves,
Henderson, Auckland

DOUBLEDAY CANADA LTD
105 Bond Street, Toronto, Ontario M5B 1Y3

Published 1991 by Doubleday
a division of Transworld Publishers Ltd

A catalogue record for this book is
available from the British Library

ISBN 0385 400403

Printed in Great Britain
by Mackays of Chatham Plc, Chatham, Kent

THE DEMON PIANO

RACHEL DIXON

Illustrated by Jon Riley

DOUBLEDAY

LONDON . NEW YORK . TORONTO . SYDNEY . AUCKLAND

For my husband, Martin

Chapter One

It was dark when Bella Blake woke, but she saw the face at once.

It hung above her bed, gleaming like a dim moon.

She said nothing, did nothing.

She felt rather surprised. It had been so long since she'd seen a ghost that she thought she'd grown out of it.

There was a dramatic piano chord. Then the face spoke.

'She's changed,' it said.

It droned on one note, like ghosts do in horror films.

'Who has?' said Bella.

'It's getting to her,' it said.

Bella's cat, Pawpaw, jumped off the bed and tried to hide under a pile of clothes.

'Who's "she"?' said Bella, sitting up. 'What do
you mean?'

The landing light clicked on.

Bella's bedroom door burst open, drowning
the face with light. Soon her mother was beside
her, cuddling her close like a baby.

Bella stared hard at the spot where the face had
been, but it had vanished.

That's typical of a ghost, she thought.

'It's all right,' said her mother. 'There's nothing
there.'

Bella didn't try to explain. Her mother would
only be upset if she told her the truth.

It had been different when she was small. Then,
her parents had been amused by her stories of the

people she saw. 'Hasn't she got a vivid imagina-
tion?' they'd say. Now, they would just think she
was mad. So Bella kept it to herself.

'It's all right,' she said, disentangling herself
from her mother's arms and snuggling down with
a convincing yawn. 'I think I had a bad dream,
but I'm all right now.'

Chapter Two

The following afternoon Bella lay on the back lawn, thinking. Three starlings were arguing in an apple tree and Pawpaw lay beside her, watching them. Bella stroked his silky head, but her thoughts were with the ghost. She should not have seen it. She had *made* herself stop seeing ghosts a long time ago, by pretending they simply weren't there.

'Bella, darling,' called her mother from a bedroom window.

The starlings flew fussily into the air, then separated like stars from a firework. Pawpaw dabbed his tongue over a paw to show he hadn't really been interested in them.

'Never mind, Paws,' said Bella. 'They were probably all feathers and bone anyway.'

'Bella,' called her mother. 'Do come up to your room. We need to talk.'

'Coming,' said Bella.

But she didn't want to go. She needed time to think, and her mother's 'talks' were usually bad news.

Some carrier-bags from smart shops were laid out on her bed.

'I thought it was time you had some new clothes,' said her mother, looking rather pink. 'So I've bought you a few things.'

'It's not my birthday, is it?' said Bella suspiciously.

It sounded rude and her mother looked unhappy.

'Please open this one first,' she said, pushing a purple bag into Bella's hand and trying to smile. 'I *know* you'll love it.'

Bella slid out a T-shirt and matching cotton trousers in a lovely bright design.

'I thought it would be good for these hot days,' said her mother. 'And you do look pretty in bright colours.'

'Thanks,' said Bella. 'It's very nice.'

Her voice still didn't sound right. She tried adding a smile as well, but it's difficult to control your face when you've got a ghost on your mind.

There were also some fun socks with bows on the side, glittery hair accessories, a pair of fluorescent Bermuda shorts and a lacy cotton blouse. Bella liked them all.

'Your dad will think I'm spoiling you,' said her mother. 'But there is a reason.'

She looked anxious for a moment, like a child.

'What did you want to talk about?' asked Bella, thinking she may as well get it over with.

Her mother looked flustered.

'I've bought your uniform too,' she said.

Bella's stomach sagged. She would have to mention *that*.

'Don't look like that, dear,' said her mother. 'Dad has gone to a lot of trouble to get you a place at Bedeside Academy.'

'I want to go to Ferndale Middle,' said Bella. 'All my friends are going there.'

'Dad and I think you'll soon make new friends at the Academy.'

She meant suitable friends. Posh friends.

'Besides, now we've moved here we are too far from Ferndale Middle.'

'You did it on purpose,' said Bella.

Her mother looked unhappy.

'Well, Dad did anyway,' said Bella. 'He never understands how I feel. He never listens.'

'I did wonder if we were doing the right thing,' said her mother, 'but Dad has persuaded me it's for the best. It'll be all right, you'll see.'

Bella was ready to leave, but there was more.

'The real reason I wanted to talk to you,' said her mother quickly, 'is to tell you about Japan.'

'Japan?'

'Yes, dear. Dad wants me to tell you that his plans for a branch of Blake's in Tokyo have all been accepted.'

She went on without pausing for breath.

'It will mean a trip over there for a month or so.'

'To Japan?' said Bella. 'That's brilliant!'

Her mother looked surprised. Pleased.

'I wasn't terribly keen on the idea so soon after we've moved,' she said. 'And of course, there was you to think of.'

'I don't mind,' said Bella. 'I bet Mrs Hathaway next door would look after Pawpaw.'

Her mother opened her mouth. And closed it again.

'Does it mean I'll miss some school?' said Bella.

'What it means,' said her mother, looking as if she wished she'd explained things better, 'is that you and Pawpaw will be going to stay at Rookhampton with Granny for the rest of the summer. You've always got on well with Granny, and that way you won't miss the start of the new term.'

Chapter Three

Bella left her light on for a long time that night. She tried to read a book, but there was too much to think about.

Pawpaw was stretched out beside her, like a furry bolster.

'We'll just have to make the most of it at Granny's, Paws,' said Bella. 'Rookhampton is boring, but Granny's all right.'

Pawpaw yawned.

'And at least we'll be together, won't we?' she said, tickling him behind his ears.

She switched off her light and turned over on to her side, but she knew she wouldn't be able to sleep.

What if the ghost came again?

Easy. She would pretend it wasn't there. She'd be ready for it this time. She would make herself go to sleep and refuse to wake up, whatever happened.

She closed her eyes, but how do you close your ears?

She pretended she had earlids, but the more she thought about it the more she was forced to listen to the sounds in the room. There was the tick-tick of her alarm clock, the creaking of the hot-water pipes, and Pawpaw's contented snores.

Suddenly a dramatic piano chord rang through the air.

Pawpaw sat up, startled.

'Don't forget,' chanted the ghost.

It was back. Bella kept her eyes tightly shut. She'd soon get rid of it that way.

But she couldn't help being a *bit* curious. The ghost must have gone to a lot of trouble to get through to someone who didn't see ghosts any more. Perhaps it had something important to tell her.

'She's different,' it said. 'Different.'

Did it mean her mother?

'All right,' said Bella, opening her eyes and speaking very slowly and clearly to try to get through to it. 'I can hear you.'

'She's different,' it said.

'Who are you talking about?' said Bella.

'It's getting to her,' chanted the ghost.

Bella sat up, crossly.

'You're just like all the others,' she said. 'You all talk in riddles. Why don't you just go away and leave me alone?'

To Bella's surprise, the face began to fade. It hadn't been that easy to get rid of them when she was younger.

'And *don't* bother coming back,' she said.

It went, and Bella was soon asleep, with Pawpaw hiding deep under her duvet.

But if she thought that was the end of the matter, Bella was wrong.

Chapter Four

Bella felt odd standing in the hall of her granny's bungalow, on her first day in Rookhampton. The village was not far away from home so, although she had visited several times, she had never stayed overnight. This time she had luggage with her and Pawpaw in his travel basket.

She didn't know what to say, so she leaned back against the cool paint of the front door and looked down at her feet. There was a balding patch on the hall carpet, shaped like South America. She traced her toe around the edge of it.

'Please don't do that, dear,' said her granny.

There was an edge to her voice. Sharp.

Bella looked up, surprised. It didn't sound like her granny and she found herself thinking of Little Red Riding Hood and the wolf.

Then her granny smiled, and the feeling passed. She looked weary though and a lot older than Bella remembered.

'I *have* been looking forward to seeing you, dear,' she said. 'But you'll have to excuse me if I don't help you unpack. It's been so noisy, it's quite worn me out. I shall have to lie down for a while.'

Pawpaw mewed from his basket, but that was the only noise Bella could hear.

'Keep him in your room, please,' said her granny as she walked away. 'You can put his food in the kitchen but take him in the back garden under supervision only.'

'Of course,' said Bella. 'I hope you feel better soon.'

But her granny had already shut her bedroom door.

'There's something funny about her,' whispered Bella to Pawpaw. 'She's changed.'

Chapter Five

As her granny was still in her room when she had finished unpacking, Bella decided to go outside. The bungalow looked out over the village green. This was a large grassy oval with three huge oak trees, one in the middle and two at the far end.

Bella found a football lying beside the middle tree. It was going a bit squashy, but it was better than nothing. She kicked it against the trunk, over and over again, not missing once until the boy appeared. He stepped out from behind the tree and deftly caught the ball as it sailed past.

'Not bad,' said Bella, waiting for him to throw it back.

'Are you trying to give me a headache?' he said. 'I was having a quiet read by this tree until you started bashing it. I thought it was a giant wood-pecker.'

He was about Bella's height with tousled fair

hair and nice brown eyes. A rolled-up comic stuck out of his jeans pocket. He smiled. It was good to see a real smile.

Bella smiled back.

'Sorry,' she said.

'Trying to get something out of your system, are you?' he said.

'Does it show?' said Bella.

He nodded and rubbed his head in mock agony. They sat by the tree, resting their backs against the rough bark.

'I'm Lee,' he said. 'What's your name?'

'Bella. I'm staying with my granny, Mrs Blake.'

'Not Old Ma Blake?' he said, blushing immediately as he realized he might have said the wrong thing. 'Sorry,' he said, 'but she's got a bit of a reputation round here.'

'Why?' said Bella. 'She's only been here for a year, since Grandpa died, but I thought she'd settled in quite well.'

'She used to be all right,' said Lee. 'But she's gone a bit funny. The local kids can't play out here for more than five minutes without her complaining about something. Has she been all right with you?'

Bella hesitated.

'I only came today,' she said. 'But she does seem very tired.'

'She's not *that* tired,' said Lee. 'Last week she told me off for resting against her front wall, *and* she's got my best football in her bungalow. She wouldn't give it back when I kicked it into her garden the other day. That's why I'm using this old thing.'

'Is it yours?' asked Bella.

'No,' he said. 'It's communal.'

'You mean it's so bad that nobody bothers to take it home?' said Bella.

'Yes,' he said. 'Something like that.'

They sat in silence for a while. Bella felt uneasy about her granny, but there was something refreshing about Lee. She liked a straight talker.

'Do you live by the green?' she said. 'I don't remember seeing you before.'

He shook his head.

'We've not been here for long. We live down on the estate, in Oak Crescent. You can't miss it. It's the road opposite the allotments.'

The sound of piano-playing wafted across the green from a house roughly opposite Mrs Blake's bungalow.

'That's good,' said Bella. 'It's Mozart, I think. Do you know who's playing?'

'A couple of old ladies live over there,' said Lee. 'They teach piano and singing. I go to see Florence, the piano lady, sometimes. My dad does a bit of gardening for her and I help if I can. She's really nice, the sort that listens. Her sister, Adelaide, teaches singing upstairs. You should hear the squawking some days. It sounds like a parrot in pain.'

'I used to play the piano,' said Bella.

'Got fed up with the practice, did you?'

'Not that,' she said. 'Someone stopped me.'

'Who?'

'My mum.'

'That's odd. Parents usually pester their kids to do things like that. Did it sound that bad?'

He grinned so she wouldn't be cross with him.

'No,' she said very quietly. 'I was pretty good actually. I loved it.'

'Couldn't she afford the lessons?' He blushed again. 'Sorry,' he said. 'I'm very nosy, aren't I?'

He seemed nice, so Bella told him a little more.

'I didn't behave well,' she said. 'Not "normally", anyway.'

'Who does?' he said, shrugging.

'They didn't try to understand me, especially my dad. I used to tell them things they didn't want to hear. The things were true, but they couldn't cope.'

'What sort of things?'

Bella didn't answer that one.

'My dad got furious with me, but my mum used to go quiet. She'd tried rewards and that hadn't worked, so she stopped my piano lessons instead.'

'That's rough,' he said. 'She could have tried something else, like . . .'

'She could have tried believing me,' said Bella. 'I think she would have, if it hadn't been for my dad.'

'Believing what?'

Bella said nothing. When you've just made a friend, however nice, you don't start telling them you used to see ghosts, especially when 'used to' is no longer the case.

'She'll get over it,' said Lee. 'I bet you get your lessons back one day.'

'Well, it certainly won't be during the next few weeks,' said Bella bitterly. 'They've gone off to Japan without me and I'm stuck here by myself.'

'Don't worry,' said Lee. 'I'll introduce you to some other kids tonight.'

'Tonight?'

'At the Nine-to-Twelves' Club. You'll be coming with your granny, won't you?'

Bella laughed.

'She's a bit old for that,' she said.

'She's standing in until they get a new leader, silly,' said Lee. 'Didn't she tell you?'

'No,' said Bella. 'But I'm not surprised they've asked her. She's run Girl Guides *and* youth clubs in her time. She's really good with kids.'

Lee gave Bella an odd look, then shrugged.

'I'm sure she is,' he said. 'I must catch her on her bad days.'

'What happened to the old leader?' said Bella, trying to change the subject.

'He was called Bill Bartlett,' said Lee.

'Scared him off, did you?' said Bella.

Lee shook his head.

'He went funny,' he said quietly. 'Then he died.'

Chapter Six

When Bella returned to the bungalow she found her granny sitting at the kitchen table, surrounded by piles of paper and thick felt-tip pens.

She looked up at Bella wearily.

'Did you forget about these, then?' she said.

'Pardon?' said Bella, wondering what she was talking about.

'The Nine-to-Twelves' Club posters,' said her granny. 'You promised to help me with them.'

'I think you forgot to ask me,' said Bella.

Her granny looked vague.

'Oh,' she said. 'It must be that wretched piano-playing. I can't think straight.'

'Surely you can't hear it from inside your bungalow,' said Bella.

'Why?' said her granny suspiciously. 'Have you been outside?'

'I just went on the green for a while,' said Bella.

'It was more than a while. I waited.'

'Sorry,' said Bella.

'I think it would have been more polite to let me know you were going out. But never mind, I'm sure you didn't *mean* to put me to so much trouble.'

Bella walked to the door. Things weren't going very well.

'I think I'll go to my room now,' she said. 'To see if Pawpaw's all right. He's not used to being shut in.'

'Before you go,' said her granny, 'there is something I would like to mention.'

There was a sharp edge to her voice.

Bella stopped in the doorway. Surprised.

'I couldn't help noticing you were talking to that boy, Lee, from the estate.'

Bella said nothing. Granny *had* known she was outside.

'He is a naughty boy,' said her granny. 'He kicks his football about. It's dangerous. I've watched him. It landed on my flowerbed last week and I was forced to confiscate it.'

'I'm sure he didn't do it on purpose,' said Bella. 'He seems very nice.'

Her granny ignored this.

'I have also found him deliberately damaging my front wall,' she said. 'On more than one occasion.'

'Why are you saying bad things about him?' said Bella hotly. 'He was only leaning on your wall. I know it. You're being mean and unfair.'

There was something wrong, thought Bella, as she returned to her room. It was as if her granny *wasn't* her granny any more.

Chapter Seven

When Bella and her grandmother arrived at the Community Hall that evening, a few club members were waiting.

Bella was glad to see that Lee was one of them.

'Hi, Bella,' he said. 'I thought I'd get here early to meet you. Good evening, Mrs Blake.'

Bella's granny did not answer. Instead she stood by the door, with her head on one side, like a blackbird listening for worms.

A tall, greasy-haired boy sat beside Lee on a plastic bin.

'Meet Gaz,' said Lee. 'He may look like a gorilla, but he's as soft as a marshmallow inside.'

'Don't tell her that,' said Gaz, pulling a long strand of chewing-gum out of his mouth, like a washing-line. 'I've got an image to keep up.'

'Shush!' said Mrs Blake.

She flapped her hand to silence them.

'There's someone in there,' she said.

They listened.

Nothing.

'I can't hear anything, Mrs Blake,' said a boy called Pritam. 'Why don't you try the door?'

'Someone's playing the piano,' said Mrs Blake.

'Barmy,' mouthed Gaz, raising his eyes.

'I don't think so, Mrs Blake,' said Pritam.

'That caretaker's been letting people in early,' she said, 'hasn't he?'

She rattled the door.

'It's locked,' said Gaz. 'I've already tried it.'

Mrs Blake jiggled her key in the lock and burst into the hall.

It was empty, but she marched down to the piano all the same.

'There's someone in here,' she said.

She climbed the steps behind the piano, on to the stage, and jabbed at the faded curtains with a roll of posters.

Gaz laughed, but Lee silenced him with a look.

'Shall we start setting things up, Mrs Blake?' said Pritam.

Mrs Blake turned to face them, standing wearily in the centre of the stage.

'She's forgotten her lines,' whispered Gaz.

'Oh, yes,' she said vaguely. 'Please do.'

Bella stood in the doorway, watching.

'Are you coming in or not, Bella?' called Lee, putting some cards and board games out on a large table.

Bella stayed where she was.

Lee walked over to her.

'Don't worry about it,' he said. 'I'm afraid she's always like that, but nobody takes any notice.'

'It isn't just that,' said Bella.

'What's up then? Are you feeling shy?'

She shook her head.

'Promise you won't laugh?'

He nodded.

'There's something bad in here, Lee.'

'You mean Gaz?' he said. 'He's all right really . . . once you get used to the smell.'

'I mean it, Lee,' said Bella quietly.

Lee looked puzzled, but before he had time to speak, Bella's granny noticed them together.

'Come and help me put up these posters please, Bella,' she called, beckoning with a thin arm.

After an hour, when fifteen members had arrived, Mrs Blake called a meeting.

'We get together like this some weeks,' said Lee, 'to decide what to do with club funds and that sort of thing.'

'Quiet, please,' said Mrs Blake, waiting for everyone to be still. 'We need to discuss the matter of the piano.'

Gaz yawned loudly.

'As you will know,' she continued, 'Bill Bartlett had planned to use both Nine-to-Twelves' Club and Youth Club funds to buy a new piano.'

'What's wrong with the one we've got?' said a thin girl called Melissa. 'I bet the new club leader can't even play the piano, and he certainly won't be able to write musicals for us like Bill Bartlett did.'

'She's right,' said Pritam. 'The one we've got is fine. *You* know that, Mrs Blake. You play it after club meetings, don't you?'

Mrs Blake looked confused, almost hunted.

'Certainly not,' she said. 'I haven't played a piano for years. But from what I've heard, there isn't much wrong with the instrument that a good clean wouldn't put right.'

Pritam looked puzzled.

'Let's keep it and use the funds for table football then,' said Melissa. 'Forget the new piano. Bill Bartlett won't know, will he?'

'The problem is,' said Mrs Blake uncomfortably, 'that Mr Bartlett ordered *and* paid for the new piano before his . . . accident.'

'He couldn't do that without the club members agreeing it,' said a boy. 'It was only at the discussion stage when he died.'

One or two others nodded their heads.

'I don't expect he gave that a thought,' said Melissa, looking round the circle to make sure everyone was listening. 'Because he went funny in the head, didn't he?'

'Melissa!' said Mrs Blake.

'Well, he did, didn't he?' said Melissa. 'He didn't know what he was doing half the time.'

'It's true,' said Pritam. 'And he was *very* odd about the piano. He snapped at us if we touched it, or told us to stop playing when there was nobody near it.'

'*And* he spoke to it,' said Melissa.

'That's enough,' snapped Mrs Blake.

'I think what Mrs Blake is trying to say,' said Lee diplomatically, 'is that as the new piano has already been paid for, there's nothing we can do about it.'

Melissa groaned.

'I vote we make the most of it then,' said Pritam.

Some others nodded.

'Thank you,' said Mrs Blake, with obvious relief.

'What happens to the old piano then?' said Melissa. 'Can we sell it and buy table football?'

'It is not ours to sell,' said Mrs Blake sharply.

'Whose is it then?' said Lee.

'It belongs to Mrs Bartlett now. Her husband brought it here when he bought a new piano for his home.'

'*She* won't want it back,' said Melissa.

'Exactly,' said Mrs Blake. 'So I told her *I* would give it a home.'

'I thought you hadn't played for years,' said Melissa.

'It's not for me,' said Mrs Blake. 'It's for Bella.'

Melissa tutted disapprovingly and one or two others exchanged looks.

Bella wished she could disappear under the floorboards.

'So how are the club funds looking at the moment?' asked Lee, before anyone could complain.

'Not very healthy,' said Mrs Blake.

'We should plan some fund-raising ideas then,' said a girl called Meena. 'My mother would help organize another sponsored swim.'

'Thank you, Meena,' said Mrs Blake. 'But we should, I think, leave any such plans to the new club leader.'

Lee bought Bella a Coke after the meeting.

'What did I tell you?' he said. 'You've got your piano back.'

'But why?' said Bella. 'Granny knows perfectly well about the piano ban.'

'Don't ask yourself why,' said Lee. 'Just enjoy it.'

Bella knew she should be pleased, but all she could feel was dread . . . as if something bad was going to come of it.

Chapter Eight

When Lee peered in through Bella's window the following afternoon, he saw Bella sitting on the edge of her bed with Pawpaw in her arms. On the floor by her feet was a box of cleaning equipment and, standing against the wall, opposite the bed, was Bill Bartlett's old piano.

The window was open a little, so Lee didn't bother to knock.

'Hi, Bella,' he said, putting his nose up to the crack.

'What *are* you doing?' said Bella. 'Granny will kill you if she sees you. You're standing on her petunias.'

'I'd better come in then,' he said.

He had the window open in a second and climbed easily into the room. Bella had to admire his cheek.

'That's never *her* cat you're cuddling,' he said, pushing the window shut behind him.

'He's mine,' said Bella.

'What's his name?'

'Pawpaw. Silly, isn't it?'

'Not really,' said Lee, 'My little sister has a rabbit called Carrot, and it doesn't look anything like one . . . apart from the green ears.'

He stroked Pawpaw gently under the chin.

'Hello, puss,' he said.

Pawpaw purred loudly.

'What's your gran doing?' he said, tickling Pawpaw behind the ears.

'She's resting,' said Bella.

'I'm not surprised,' said Lee. 'She was in a bit of a state when I got to the Community Hall today.'

'What were you doing there?' said Bella.

'Gaz's dad asked a few kids to help get Bill Bartlett's piano on to the trailer.'

'Only Pritam and Gaz were with him when he delivered it,' she said.

'He asked me too,' said Lee. 'And I was the first there, but after your gran went for me I had to unvolunteer myself.'

'What did you do to her?' said Bella. 'She was all right when she left.'

'Nothing.'

He went pink.

'Yes you did,' said Bella accusingly. 'You're blushing.'

'I saw her . . .' he said, 'doing something weird.'

Bella wasn't sure she wanted to hear what he had seen, but he carried on all the same.

'She was kneeling in front of the piano,' he said. 'I'm not kidding, Bella.'

'So?' said Bella. 'Perhaps she'd lost something, or perhaps she was checking to see if it had castors.'

'That's what I thought,' said Lee, 'until I heard her talking to it.'

'Granny wouldn't talk to a piano,' said Bella, hoping it wasn't true.

'I was surprised too,' said Lee.

'Could you hear what she was saying?'

'Not really,' said Lee. 'She shut up when she saw me. She looked pretty shaky though. I went to help her up and that's when she went for me.'

'What do you mean?'

'She started whacking me on the leg with her handbag. If Gaz and co. hadn't arrived I might have lost the use of my leg completely.'

'It looks all right to me,' said Bella. 'And it didn't stop you climbing through my window.'

'True,' he said, grinning. 'But she had me worried for a minute.'

Bella looked worried too, so Lee changed the subject.

'It's a funny old piano, isn't it?' he said, walking over and tracing his finger around the carved panels. 'I've never seen another one with a candle still stuck on the front. You'd better not use it. It might set the music on fire.'

He picked off a dribble of wax. 'Got to clean it up, have you?'

'Yes,' said Bella. 'It's filthy, but I can't complain, can I? I've got a piano again and Granny has even offered to pay for lessons.'

'I know,' said Lee. 'With Florence Eisenhandler. She told my dad.'

'It's odd though,' said Bella, 'because I know Granny can't really afford it.'

'I'll help you clean it if you like,' said Lee.

The top of the piano was open so he looked inside.

'Phaw,' he said. 'It smells pretty fusty. And some idiot's chucked a crisp bag in there.'

He pulled out the bag, threw it expertly into Bella's waste-bin and closed the piano lid.

'Ugh!' he said. 'It's got rings from coffee cups

on the top. We'd better get to work on it.'

Bella pushed Pawpaw down, but seemed reluctant to move herself.

'Come on,' said Lee. 'It's not going to clean itself, is it?'

As Bella walked over, Lee opened the keyboard lid.

The keys were stained and dusty.

'They're like teeth,' said Bella, shivering. 'They're grinning at us.'

'If I had teeth as bad as that, I'd give up smiling for good,' said Lee.

They worked on the keys with a dot of creamy bath cleaner on a sponge, then brushed away the cobwebs under the keyboard, prised a rusty drawing-pin out of the lid, cleared old programmes from behind the lower panelling and polished the pedals.

It looked much better.

Lee rummaged in the box of cleaning things and pulled out a small bottle.

'This is what it needs now,' he said. 'Hideaway Scratch Cover.'

He pulled out an old tea towel. 'I'll put it on with this,' he said. 'And you can polish it off with a duster.'

The piano looked quite smart when they had finished.

Pawpaw jumped on to the keyboard lid to investigate. He was obviously impressed and decided it was now a suitable place to sleep. He curled up as neatly as he could, with his fluffy tail already twitching in anticipation of a good mouse-catching dream.

'Too bad,' said Lee. 'I was going to ask you to play me a tune.'

'Another time,' said Bella.

'Saved by the cat,' said Lee. 'How does it sound anyway? I couldn't really tell from the noise we made cleaning the keys.'

'I don't know,' said Bella. 'I haven't tried it yet.'

'Why not?' he said. 'I thought you couldn't wait to play again.'

Bella shrugged.

There was a noise from the hall.

'I'd better beat it before your gran finds me,' said Lee, opening the window and leaping deftly out again. 'See you.'

As she watched Lee go, Bella heard a scrabbling noise behind her.

She turned.

Pawpaw was standing erect on the piano with his eyes wide and his fur sticking out like a feather duster. And, as Bella watched, he jumped agitatedly to the floor, yowling as if his paws had been burnt.

Chapter Nine

Lee was by the middle oak tree when Bella walked across the green the following morning.

'Hi, Bella,' he said. 'It's your first piano lesson this morning, isn't it?'

'Yes,' she said. 'In five minutes. What are you up to?'

'Not a lot,' he said, picking a daisy and twirling it between his fingers. 'I try to get out as much as I can. I've got at least a hundred sisters at home, all of them younger than me, so I come out for a bit of peace.'

'How many sisters?' said Bella accusingly.

'Two,' he said, grinning. 'But it feels like a hundred on a bad day.'

Bella leaned on the tree, pulling at its knobbly bark with her fingers.

'You're nervous about your lesson, aren't you?' said Lee.

'A bit.'

'Don't worry. You'll like Florence,' he said.
'And I heard you practising your scales just now.
That ought to help.'

'I'm a bit rusty,' said Bella. 'It's over a year
since I played.'

'What do you think of the piano?'

'It's OK,' said Bella unenthusiastically.

'That good?' laughed Lee.

'It needs tuning,' said Bella.

As she spoke, Bella turned towards the bungalow. She put her head on one side, puzzled.

'You can hear for yourself,' she said. 'Granny's
playing it. She's brilliant, isn't she? I'd no idea she
could play as well as that.'

'You must have better ears than me,' said Lee.
'I can't hear a note.'

Florence was waiting in the doorway when Bella
arrived. She was a small lady. Her hair was of the
finest silvery-white and shone in the sun like
dewy cobwebs. Brown wrinkles fanned out
around her gentle grey eyes, but though she was
old she did not look frail.

'You must be Bella,' she said, smiling.

Her voice was like silver.

'Come in, dear,' she said. 'I've been looking
forward to meeting you.'

She drew Bella into her music-room. It was light and airy, with beautiful pieces of furniture, lovely rugs and tall pot plants. She gently pushed Bella down into a deep, soft armchair and put a record on her old-fashioned gramophone.

'Chopin, my dear,' she said, sitting herself. 'Let us listen and learn.'

She closed her eyes and rocked a little as the music played. Only when the needle had clicked a few times in the middle of the record did she open her eyes.

'Now, my dear,' she said. 'I should very much like to hear *you* play.'

She indicated an open book on the piano.

'I gather from your granny that this might be suitable.'

The piece, *A Prelude* by Pachulski, was a perfect choice.

'Key?' said Florence.

'C Minor,' said Bella, excited to discover that she had not forgotten everything.

'Start when you're ready, dear,' said Florence. '*Andante espressivo.*'

Bella began. Her playing was shaky at first. Her fingers felt stiff and her ankle quivered above the pedal. But little by little her body relaxed, the room receded and the music took over, leading her through to its final ritardando.

'You have a real feeling for the music, dear,' said Florence, after a moment's silence. 'There is naturally some work to be done, but I think you will enjoy learning.'

She rose gracefully.

'And now I would like to show you my garden.'

She opened the french window.

'Adelaide and I used to tend it ourselves, but we have had to get a little help from Lee's father recently.'

The garden was lovely. A blackbird sang from a cherry tree and a pupil, upstairs in Adelaide's room, practised her arpeggios squeakily.

'It's very pretty out here,' said Bella.

'And peaceful,' said Florence. 'I could stay out here all day, but I think we should try some duets now, don't you?'

'Oh, yes please,' said Bella. 'I'd love to.'

Bella played well. The duets were great fun and she really wanted to please Florence.

Everything was perfect until a dramatic piano chord rang out in the middle of one of the pieces.

Bella stopped, startled, but Florence carried on playing. She hadn't heard it.

Then the face appeared. It was suddenly there on the duet book, quavering about like a reflection on ripply water. Bella tried to ignore it. She

managed to find her place again, but it was
difficult to read the music through a ghost's head.
She willed it to go away, but the ripples steadied
and the mouth spoke.

'She needs help,' it chanted. 'Upstairs.'

The face disappeared as quickly as it had come,
but Bella was not free. She felt a sharp jab in her
chest, a nasty tight feeling. She tried to keep
playing but was forced to stop, doubled up in
pain. Florence stopped too, obviously puzzled.

'I'm sorry, Miss Eisenhandler,' said Bella. 'I
don't think I can play any more today.'

She avoided looking into those kind grey eyes
and stiffly gathered up the music Florence had
given her.

'I must go now,' she said. 'You'll want to get to your sister.'

And as Bella opened the front door to leave, she was not surprised to hear a young voice shouting from the top of the stairs: 'Miss Eisenhandler! Oh, please come quickly. Your sister has collapsed.'

Bella ran. She wanted to get away desperately, but her legs felt too heavy. She reached the gate, where a hand caught hold of her arm, jolting her to a halt.

It was Lee.

'Where are you going?' he said. 'You must have heard the girl. She needs help.'

'I'm not going back in there,' cried Bella. 'Let me go!'

'I don't believe I'm hearing this,' said Lee, letting go of her arm as if it were something nasty. 'Run away if you like, but I'm going in there.'

He was right, of course, and Bella followed him.

Later, as Adelaide was being lifted into the ambulance, Florence took Bella's hand.

'You knew, didn't you, dear?' she said. 'How frightening for you.'

'Knew what?' said Lee.

Chapter Ten

Back at the oak tree, Bella sat on the grass and hugged her knees up close to her chest. Lee sat down beside her. He picked a dandelion clock and swished it in the air to let the tiny parachutes fly.

'What did Florence mean about you knowing?' he said.

Bella said nothing.

'You can tell *me*,' he said. 'I am your friend, aren't I?'

Bella shrugged.

'I knew about Adelaide,' she said, staring across the green to avoid Lee's eyes. 'A ghost told me.'

'Never!' said Lee, but from the tone of her voice, he had a funny feeling she might be telling the truth.

'Was it in Florence's place?' he asked, his eyes gleaming at the thought.

Bella nodded. Lee wanted to believe her.

'Are you sure?' he said. 'You're not having me on, are you?'

'It was nothing,' said Bella flatly. 'I used to see them a lot when I was small.'

Lee was silent for a moment. This was really weird.

'That wasn't why you lost your piano lessons, was it?' he said.

Bella nodded.

'I made myself stop seeing ghosts after that,' she said, 'Until this one started pestering me.'

'You mean you've seen it before?'

'It appeared in my bedroom at home. It took me by surprise the first time, but I was ready for it after that.'

'What did you do?' said Lee. 'Zap it with your slippers?'

'I told it to push off,' said Bella. 'And I thought it had worked.'

'Until this morning,' said Lee.

'Yes,' said Bella grimly. 'Somehow it's managed to follow me to Rookhampton.'

'Perhaps it was in the Community Hall the other night,' said Lee. 'You didn't want to come in, remember?'

'Perhaps,' said Bella.

'What does it look like?'

'Just a head . . . a man's head, gleaming like a lamp.'

'I thought ghosts looked like sheets with people underneath.'

Bella managed a smile.

'They *never* look like that,' she said.

'And what does it do?'

'It hangs there and chants.'

'What does it say?'

'Rubbish mostly, but it made more sense today,' said Bella. 'It said, "She needs help. Upstairs." '

'Couldn't Florence see it?'

'No,' said Bella. 'It was right there on the duet book. I could hardly see through it, but Florence just carried on playing.'

'So why didn't you go upstairs?' said Lee. 'Why did you run away?'

'I'm not sure,' said Bella. 'I can't remember. I felt a pain in my chest and I couldn't think straight . . . I think I tried to tell Florence that her sister needed her, but everything went fuzzy and I panicked.'

'You shouldn't have run away,' said Lee. 'You've got powers that might have helped Adelaide.'

Bella tried to remember what she had felt in

there . . . the pain and the panic.

It came back to her too easily, like a knife stab.

'I remember now,' she said. 'I didn't go up there because I knew it would be no use. The ghost said she needed help, but as soon as I felt the pain, I knew it was too late.'

Lee was silent for a moment. Then he put his arm round her.

'That must have been awful,' he said. 'I'm sorry I was cross with you.'

'That's all right,' she said numbly. 'I can't tell you how good it feels to have someone believe me for a change. I sometimes wonder if I'm crazy.'

'I don't think you're crazy,' said Lee. 'Not very, but your gran will be if she sees us sitting here like this!'

Chapter Eleven

It was Saturday when Lee saw Bella again. He was playing cricket at the far end of the green with some children from the Nine-to-Twelves' Club, when they noticed her.

'Take a look at Bella Blake,' said Gaz, pointing his bat in the direction of Mrs Blake's bungalow. 'Is she going barmy like her gran, or what?'

Bella was crouching on the pavement by her granny's front wall.

'She's hiding,' said Meena.

'So would I, if I had a gran like that,' said Pritam.

'There's something wrong,' said Lee.

'Serves her right, if you ask me,' said Melissa, throwing the ball expertly from hand to hand. 'We'd have been able to get table football if it hadn't been for her.'

'I'm going over,' said Lee.

'Please yourself,' said Melissa. 'But *we're* not stopping.'

Nobody argued with Melissa. She was lethal with a cricket ball in her hands.

Lee called out before he reached Bella, so as not to startle her.

'Get down,' she hissed, flapping her hand at him. 'There's someone in there.'

Lee crouched down and waddled across the road to join her.

'In where?'

'In my granny's.'

'How do you know?'

She gave him a strange look.

'I can hear them, stupid.'

Lee listened carefully.

'I can't hear anything,' he said.

'Someone's playing the piano, idiot,' said Bella.

'And I know it's not Granny this time. She's gone to get some flowers for Florence.'

Lee felt uneasy. Like last time, there *was* no playing.

'Are you sure it's coming from in there?' he said.

'Yes,' said Bella. 'And it's driving me mad.'

'It could be a radio,' said Lee.

'It's somebody playing Bill Bartlett's piano,' said Bella. 'And I intend to stop them. Are you coming with me or not?'

Lee opened his mouth.

'You're not scared, are you?' she said.

'Of course not,' he said.

'Don't worry,' said Bella, producing a rolled-up copy of *Fast Forward*. 'I've got this.'

'Oh, that's all right then,' said Lee, hoping nobody was watching.

They crawled up the drive towards the front door. Lee could feel the pebbles rasping against the knees of his new jeans and knew his mum would kill him if he'd spoilt them.

'Stay down while I unlock the door,' said Bella. 'Then follow me.'

It was cool in the hall, and silent. Lee was sure there was nothing wrong, but he followed Bella all the same. She said she could hear something.

She was his friend and he had to believe her.

As Bella opened her bedroom door, Pawpaw burst out into the hall. His fur stood on end and his eyes were wide. Bella strode in, brandishing the *Fast Forward*.

Lee followed. They stood together in the middle of the room, in silence. There was nobody else there, the piano lid was shut and there was no music.

'It's stopped,' said Bella. 'Can you hear anything?'

'Not a note,' said Lee.

'There must be someone in here,' said Bella.

She lay down beside the bed and peered underneath.

'You check the wardrobe,' she said.

This was getting silly, but Bella obviously needed to be reassured.

'Nothing in here,' Lee said cheerfully, stepping inside just to make sure.

There was a dramatic piano chord.

'Not *you*,' said Bella crossly.

'I beg your pardon?' said Lee, peering out from behind her school blazer.

What he saw made him feel sick.

Bella was staring into the air, at a place just above the piano. She wasn't talking to him at all.

She was talking to a greenish face that hung there, gleaming like a moon.

'I thought I told you to go away,' said Bella to the face. 'I know you did your best for Adelaide, but that doesn't mean I feel any differently about ghosts.'

Lee decided to stay in the wardrobe. He would have liked to pull the door shut too, but as he didn't dare to put his hand out to reach it, he had to make do with shutting his eyes.

'It's getting to you,' chanted the face.

The voice was quite musical, thought Lee. Almost operatic.

'The only thing that's getting to me is *you*,' said Bella. 'I should have guessed it was you playing. It's been driving me crazy. I keep practising for hours in the hope that you'll get fed up with waiting.'

'That's what it wants. It wants to be played,' said the face. 'I should know. It did it to me.'

There was something vaguely familiar about that voice, thought Lee. He opened his eyes a crack. The face was still there. It was an anxious face. Hunted.

And Lee had seen the face before.

'You're not trying to tell me the piano has been

making that row all by itself, are you?' said Bella. 'What rubbish.'

Lee tried to get Bella's attention.

'Who are you anyway?' said Bella. 'And what are you up to?'

'It's Bill,' said Lee, stepping out of the wardrobe in a sudden burst of bravery. 'It's Bill Bartlett.'

The face disappeared.

Bella looked round, startled.

'Could you see it?' she said.

Lee nodded. His legs suddenly sagged, like bendy drinking straws.

'Here,' said Bella, taking his arm. 'Sit on the bed. I suppose ghosts can be a bit of a shock if you're not used to them.'

Bella fetched Lee a drink and Pawpaw ventured back into the room. He jumped up on to Lee's lap, nuzzled his face to say hello and curled up into a tight ball.

'He likes you,' said Bella.

'He's not so keen on spooks though,' said Lee.

'There's something in here that scares him a lot more than ghosts,' said Bella. 'And if that really was the ghost of Bill Bartlett, I think I might know what it is.'

Lee looked puzzled.

'You heard what he said about the piano, didn't you?'

'Not really,' said Lee. 'I was too busy being brave.'

'He said, "It wants to be played . . . It did it to me," ' said Bella.

'That's ridiculous,' said Lee. 'He makes it sound as if pianos can think.'

'It does sound a bit weird,' said Bella. 'But it would explain a lot about Bill Bartlett's odd behaviour, wouldn't it?'

'He did go a bit funny about it.'

'Pritam said he was obsessed with it,' said Bella. 'According to the club members, Bill Bartlett heard the piano when nobody else could. He also played it when he didn't mean to.'

'And Melissa saw him talking to it,' said Lee. 'He was crazy, Bella, and his ghost is too.'

'Maybe,' said Bella. 'And maybe not.'

She stared across at the piano.

'But if by any chance it *is* true that Bill Bartlett's piano can think, it needn't get the idea it's going to use its tricks to make *me* play,' she said. 'I shall play when *I* want to or not at all.'

Chapter Twelve

It was as Lee was about to leave that the piano started playing again. It was so loud that it hurt Bella's head.

'Let's get out of here,' she said, holding her hands over her ears.

'Why are you shouting?' said Lee.

Pawpaw ran across the room and scratched at the door.

'The music,' said Bella. 'It's hurting my ears.'

Lee could hear no music.

'It is *not* playing,' he said, trying to make Bella look at him.

'It *is*,' shouted Bella. 'If you're my friend, get me out of here.'

Lee pulled the doorhandle. It was stuck.

'Oh no!' said Bella. 'It's trapped us in here.'

'Don't be silly,' said Lee. 'It's jammed, that's all.'

He pulled hard, but it would not open.

'Easy,' he said, wishing he wasn't beginning to panic. 'We'll get out of the window.'

He pulled the window catch. It was stuck. And worse still, he could see Mrs Blake walking up the front drive.

'It's your gran,' he said. 'She'll go mad if she finds me in here.'

Bella was doubled up on the piano stool, as if in pain.

'Quick!' said Lee, trying the wardrobe door as a last resort. 'Let's hide in here.'

It too was stuck.

He would probably have pulled Bella under the bed if Pawpaw hadn't beaten them to it.

It was too late. Mrs Blake was in the hall.

Never mind, thought Lee. At least she won't be able to get in.

The doorhandle slipped silently down and Lee watched in horror as the door slid open.

Bella opened her eyes.

'Thank goodness,' she said. 'It's stopped.'

Her granny stepped into the room.

'Hello, Mrs Blake,' said Lee. 'I was just going.'

'I should think you are,' said Bella's granny, frowning so hard that her thin eyebrows met in the middle like knitting-needles. 'I'd like to know

who invited you into my home in the first place.'

'I did,' said Bella.

Her granny sniffed.

'At least he didn't stop you doing your piano practice,' she said. 'I could hear it from outside. I'd no idea you were so advanced.'

She turned to Lee, just as he was about to slip out of the door.

'She's good, isn't she?' she said.

'Very good,' said Lee uneasily. He looked at his wrist. 'Gosh,' he said. 'Is that really the time? I must be off.'

His watch was at the mender's, but he doubted if Bella or Mrs Blake had noticed.

As he left the bungalow, so did Pawpaw,

beating Lee to the front gate by a whisker.

Bella did not notice either of them leave. Instead she stared at her granny.

'You heard it?' she said. 'The playing?'

'Of course I did,' said Mrs Blake. 'And I'm glad the piano is getting plenty of use . . . it *was* you, wasn't it?'

Bella nodded. She daren't tell her the truth.

Mrs Blake ran her hand over the piano, as if she was stroking an animal.

'It *needs* to be played. I knew it the moment I touched it.'

She gave Bella a sharp look and Bella wondered if she knew more than she was letting on.

'You will make full use of it, won't you, dear?' she said. 'I'd love to keep playing it myself, but I'm not as young as I was.'

Bella watched her granny patting the piano, and began to understand.

'Of course, Granny,' she said obediently. 'I'll start right away.'

Chapter Thirteen

It was raining hard when Lee arrived at the
Nine-to-Twelves' Club on Tuesday. Gaz, Meena
and Pritam were waiting outside, unsuccessfully
huddled under one umbrella.

'I should come out from under there, Gaz,' said
Lee. 'You could do with a hairwash.'

'No way,' said Gaz. 'It's taken me months to
perfect this style.'

'Where's Mrs Blake?' said Pritam.

'It's not like her to be late,' said Meena.

Lee felt a stab of anxiety. He hadn't seen Bella since Saturday.

'Here she comes,' said Gaz. 'Or is it Batgran?'

A large umbrella approached. Under it strode Mrs Blake, her huge black raincoat flapping out behind her like wings.

'I'm sorry to keep you waiting on a night like this,' she said breathlessly.

'That's all right,' said Meena.

'Where's Bella?' said Lee.

Mrs Blake gave him a sharp look.

'What's it to you?' she said.

'Can we let Mrs Blake unlock the door, Lee?' said Pritam. 'We haven't all got posh kagouls like you.'

Once inside the hall, Lee tackled Mrs Blake again.

'Is Bella coming tonight?' he said.

'No,' said Mrs Blake.

She shook her raincoat over the mat. Raindrops ran down it like tears.

'Is she ill?' said Lee.

'It's no business of yours whether she's ill or not,' said Mrs Blake, trying to walk into the hall.

'I'm her friend,' said Lee, standing in front of her.

Mrs Blake walked round him as if she were avoiding something nasty on the pavement.

'I should leave it, Lee,' said Pritam. 'Let's have a game of cards.'

How could Pritam know what was best? He didn't know about Bill Bartlett's warning. Lee had been able to think of little else since Saturday and he knew he should have had the courage to check before now that Bella was all right. He had been praying that she would turn up tonight and that everything would be back to normal.

But she wasn't there, and Lee had an awful feeling that something was very wrong.

'No thanks, Pritam,' he said. 'I have to see Bella.'

Lee ran straight to the bungalow, not noticing puddles, not caring when water sloshed into his shoes.

He could hear piano music as soon as he got there, scales playing up and down, up and down. He felt scared. Was he hearing things, like Bella had?

He pressed his nose up against her window and dared himself to open his eyes.

It was Bella.

He knocked on the wet window.

'Bella, it's me!' he called.

Bella did not seem to hear him. She stared straight ahead and carried on playing.

'Bella!' shouted Lee. 'Let me in.'

There was something wrong. She looked odd and stiff, as if she were in a trance.

Lee slipped over wet soil to the front door and rang the bell.

The playing continued.

He hammered on the door, but it was no good. Perhaps the ghost had been right. Perhaps the piano was sending her crazy. What was he going to do?

He went back to the window, determined to get her attention.

'Bella!' he shouted. 'Can you hear me?'

There was no reaction. The scales continued. Lee wasn't musical, but he could tell she wasn't playing normally. It sounded more like a machine, and she looked more like a puppet.

'Look at me,' said Lee. 'Look at me *now*.'

Bella turned her head towards the window. Her eyes stared in Lee's direction, but she did not seem to see him.

'It's me,' said Lee. 'STOP PLAYING!'

Bella turned her head back to the piano again,

and her hands kept playing.

'That piano's crazy,' shouted Lee. 'It's doing you harm.'

But however hard Lee tried, he could get no further response from her.

There was no point in staying.

'Don't worry, Bella,' he called, hoping she could hear. 'I'll get you out of this somehow.'

Back at the club, Lee drew Pritam to one side.

'I need help,' he said. 'Bella's in danger. We've got to get her out of that bungalow.'

'Shouldn't you call the fire brigade or something?' said Pritam, looking worried.

'It's nothing like that,' said Lee.

'What is it like?' said Pritam suspiciously.

'I can't explain,' said Lee. 'You'll have to trust me. And please hurry.'

Mrs Blake noticed them leaving.

'You needn't think you can sneak away without paying your subs,' she said.

'We'll be back in a minute, Mrs Blake,' said Pritam. 'We want to get some atmosphere for our paintings.'

It was still pouring outside.

'This had better be for real, Lee,' said Pritam. 'I

haven't recovered from the last soaking yet.'

They were nearing the bungalow when they saw Bella splashing towards them.

'Bella!' called Lee. 'Are you all right?'

'Hi,' said Bella. 'Aren't you going to the club?'

'We've just come from there,' said Pritam crossly. 'To rescue *you*.'

'You look as if you're the one who needs rescuing,' said Bella. 'Want to share my umbrella?'

'How did you get out, Bella?' said Lee.

'Through the door, of course,' she said.

As she spoke, Lee noticed something very odd about Bella's voice, something almost mechanical, as if she were not in control of what she was saying.

Pritam did not notice.

'Very funny, Lee,' he said. 'I'll get you for this.'

But Lee wasn't laughing.

Chapter Fourteen

Lee splashed straight home and lay crossly on his bed, staring at the ceiling.

'That's the last time I have anything to do with Bella Blake,' he said. 'She's trouble, that girl.'

An irritating strand of cobweb hung from the ceiling, heavy with dust. He closed his eyes so he would not have to see it.

There was a dramatic piano chord.

It jangled through the air, just like the one he had heard from Bella's wardrobe.

His stomach flopped.

'It's you, isn't it?' he said. 'Bill Bartlett's ghost.'

He had meant to sound brave, but his voice came out in a sort of squeak.

'She needs help,' chanted a voice.

Lee opened his eyes. It was there all right — a greenish head, hanging next to the strand of cobweb.

'Hello,' he said.

'She must get rid of it,' chanted the ghost. 'It's the only way. I tried, but it was too late.'

Lee took a deep breath and cleared his throat.

'If it's Bella you're talking about, I think you've come to the wrong house,' he said.

'It's getting to her,' chanted the ghost. 'She won't hear me.'

'That's not my problem,' said Lee, feeling a little braver.

'She must get rid of it.'

'You mean the piano, don't you?' said Lee.

'She needs help.'

The voice was on a much higher note this time. Lee presumed that was how ghosts showed they were worried.

'What do you expect *me* to do?' said Lee. 'I can't walk in there and say, "Excuse me, I've just come to take your piano away," can I?'

'She needs help.'

'It would be too heavy, for one thing. And besides, I'm not having anything else to do with Bella Blake.'

'She needs help.'

The voice was really high this time, almost falsetto.

'OK, OK,' said Lee. 'But will you *please* tell me what I'm supposed to do about it?'

There was no answer.

The ghost had disappeared.

Chapter Fifteen

When Florence Eisenhandler's doorbell rang on Thursday morning, she was not expecting to see Lee.

'Hello, dear,' she said. 'I thought it must be Bella. She knows I've started teaching again this morning, but she's late for her lesson. Did you see her on the green?'

Lee shook his head.

'I've come to weed the rosebed,' he said. 'If that's all right.'

'Of course it is,' said Florence, 'and it's lovely to see you.'

Lee looked different, she thought, as she drew him into the house. Sad.

'I'm sorry about . . . you know,' he said.

'About Adelaide?' she said. 'It is all right to mention her name, you know. In fact, I'd rather people did talk about her.'

'Dad said the funeral was lovely,' said Lee.

He blushed. What a silly thing to say.

'It was, dear,' said Florence gently.

The phone shrilled, cutting through the air like a knife.

'Why not pour yourself a glass of lemonade, while I answer this,' said Florence.

She soon joined him and they sat outside on creaky wicker chairs. The air was heavy with the scent of flowers and sparrows chirruped in the hedge.

'That was Mrs Blake,' she said, looking puzzled. 'Bella won't be coming today.'

'Is she all right?' said Lee.

'It was very odd, Lee,' said Florence. 'Mrs Blake told me that Bella was ill in bed, but I'm sure I could hear piano-playing in the background.'

Lee choked on his drink.

'I thought it might be the radio at first,' said Florence, 'but it sounded like someone practising scales.'

'It might have been a children's music programme,' said Lee.

But he knew it wasn't.

It was Bella. Bill Bartlett's piano was forcing her to play again.

He felt awful. Guilty. He should have helped her.

'Is there something wrong, Lee?' said Florence.

'No,' he said.

'I know you're upset about Adelaide, but there's something else, isn't there?'

'No,' he said, shaking his head to try and make it look more convincing.

'Do you want to talk about it?' she said.

'I can't,' he said, wishing he didn't feel like crying. 'It's too weird. You won't believe me.'

'Try me,' she said firmly.

So he did.

Florence sat in silence for a long time after Lee had finished his story.

'Poor Bella,' she said eventually.

'You believe me?'

'I do, Lee,' she said. 'Bella is an unusual child. She knew about Adelaide. I've no doubt strange things happen around her, though it is hard to imagine a musical instrument that is capable of doing harm. They have always seemed like treasures to me.'

'You don't think Bella could be imagining things, do you?' said Lee. 'I know the ghost was there, because I saw it. But can you believe in a piano that thinks?'

'Bella obviously sees things more deeply than you and me,' said Florence. 'If she says the piano has these powers, we must try to believe her.'

'What I don't understand then,' said Lee, 'is why Bella takes any notice of it. She told me that when she was younger, she managed to get rid of ghosts by ignoring them. Why couldn't she do that with the piano?'

'I think she could be protecting someone else,' said Florence.

'Not Bill Bartlett?' said Lee. 'It's too late for him.'

'No,' said Florence. 'I think Bella is protecting her grandmother. You have told me yourself about Mrs Blake's strange behaviour, and it all seems to centre around that piano.'

'You're right,' said Lee. 'Just like it did with Bill Bartlett.'

'Poor woman,' said Florence. 'I expect she was the first person to play it after he died.'

'But she didn't have to pass it on to Bella, did she?' said Lee bitterly.

'She probably had no idea what she was doing,' said Florence. 'She isn't as perceptive as Bella.'

'She's a nasty old woman,' said Lee. 'Bella's going to end up like Bill Bartlett because of her. That piano's going to kill Bella . . . We've got to do something, Miss Eisenhandler.'

'It might help if we knew what made it behave so badly in the first place,' said Florence calmly. 'Do you think it possible that it was jealous of Bill Bartlett's new piano?'

'*I* don't know,' said Lee. 'And even if it *was*, Bill Bartlett can hardly take it back now, can he?'

'It sounds as if things had gone too far for that, even *before* he died,' said Florence.

'We've got to get rid of it,' said Lee. 'That's what his ghost told me.'

'I think I agree,' said Florence, 'but how?'

Chapter Sixteen

A few minutes later, Lee and Florence were standing outside Mrs Blake's bungalow. Inside, someone was playing the piano.

'That doesn't sound like Bella,' said Florence, ringing the doorbell. 'It's too mechanical.'

'Bella won't come,' said Lee.

'But it's not like Mrs Blake to ignore the doorbell,' said Florence, ringing again.

'I bet she's gone out,' said Lee angrily, 'and left Bella in there.'

He scrambled over the flowerbed and peered in at the window.

'It's her all right,' he said.

Florence stepped carefully over the petunias to see for herself.

Bella sat upright, with hands stiff and white like polished ivory. While her fingers played mechanically, her mouth opened and closed jerkily, as if she were a talking doll.

'I didn't realize it would be as bad as this,' said Florence.

'Bella!' cried Lee, rapping on the window. 'It's me. I've brought Miss Eisenhandler. Let us in. We can help you.'

Bella carried on playing.

They turned away, to see Mrs Blake staring at them from the other side of the garden wall.

'Miss Eisenhandler,' she said indignantly. 'You are standing in my flowerbed. I've come to expect that sort of behaviour from Lee, but I *never* expected it from you.'

Lee tried to replant a pink petunia with the toe of his trainer, but it was beyond help.

'I do apologize,' said Florence. 'We were trying to get Bella's attention.'

'Bella,' said Mrs Blake, striding up her drive to the front door, 'is *not* to be disturbed.'

She let herself into the bungalow and slammed the door.

'Oh dear,' said Florence. 'This is going to be even harder than I thought.'

Chapter Seventeen

Melissa, Gaz and Pritam arrived at Lee's house together on Friday lunchtime.

'We got your message,' said Pritam.

'But it had better be important,' said Melissa.

'Yeah,' said Gaz. 'I'm starving and it's fish and chips today.'

'We've got a brilliant idea to discuss with you,' said Lee.

'We?' said Melissa suspiciously.

'Miss Eisenhandler and me,' he said. 'Come in and meet her.'

They followed Lee into his living-room.

'Hello,' said Florence. 'We haven't met, but I recognize you all. I often watch you playing out on the green.'

'This is Melissa and that's Gaz,' said Pritam politely.

'And he's Pritam,' said Gaz.

They all sat.

'Got anything to eat?' said Gaz, opening a pack of rabbit food he had found down the side of the chair and sniffing at it.

'Shut up, Gaz,' said Melissa. 'Let's find out what this is about.'

'Lee and I want to arrange a little surprise for somebody,' said Florcncc. 'And we would appreciate your help.'

'Wicked!' said Gaz. 'I love surprises.'

'It depends what sort of surprise it is,' said Melissa.

'Quite so,' said Florence.

'Give her a chance to tell us, Melissa,' said Pritam.

'I am planning to give a surprise gift to a friend,' said Florence.

'Why do you need our help?' asked Pritam.

'Because it's rather a big gift,' said Lee.

'How big?' said Gaz.

'Piano-sized actually,' said Lee.

'Hey!' said Gaz. 'Whatever is it?'

'A piano, you dummy,' said Melissa.

'And who is it for?' said Pritam.

'Bella Blake,' said Florence.

'Not another one!' said Melissa. 'She seems to get all the pianos around here.'

'My sister Adelaide always wanted her Bechstein to go to a pupil of promise and . . . I feel Bella is the ideal person,' said Florence.

Melissa pulled a face.

'It's not long since Miss Eisenhandler lost her sister,' said Lee, 'so I think we should try to make this as easy for her as possible.'

'I was sorry to hear about that, Miss Eisenhandler,' said Pritam. 'I don't mind helping.'

'It will only need to be moved round the green,' said Lee.

'My dad would lend us the trolley,' said Gaz.

'And what will happen about Bill Bartlett's piano?' said Pritam.

'That's the other part of the job,' said Lee. 'It

will have to be moved out. And of course, Bella will have to be kept out of the way.'

He made it sound so ordinary.

'Perhaps we can sell Bill Bartlett's piano for the club after all,' said Melissa sniffily. 'Bella should never have had it in the first place.'

'The trouble is,' said Lee, 'that it can't really be sold. Mrs Blake was going to have to get rid of it anyway because . . .'

'Because of moths in the felts,' said Florence.

'And the woodworm,' added Lee.

'In fact, I'm afraid it would probably be a good idea if it were destroyed completely,' said Florence. 'Before it affects anything else.'

'What a pity,' said Pritam. 'I suppose we'll have to take it to the tip.'

'But that's miles away,' said Gaz. 'I can get the trolley, but I don't think my dad will let us use the van again.'

'It *is* too far,' agreed Florence.

'Out of the question,' said Lee.

'In fact,' said Florence, 'Lee and I were hoping one of you might have an idea how to dispose of it closer to home.'

'We could blow it up in Mrs Blake's front garden,' said Gaz, grinning enthusiastically.

'Don't be silly,' said Pritam.

'You're right,' said Gaz, giggling. 'It might kill her petunias.'

'Shut up both of you,' said Melissa. 'I've just remembered something.'

'Shall I call the newspapers?' said Lee sarcastically.

'There's *another* piano in Rookhampton that needs to be disposed of, isn't there?' said Melissa.

'That's hardly front-page news,' said Lee.

'What piano is that, dear?' said Florence.

'The Sunday School one, of course,' said Melissa. 'We passed the piano from the Community Hall on to them when Bill Bartlett gave us his. They haven't managed to get rid of their old one yet. My mother runs the Sunday School and she says it's getting in the way.'

'Brilliant,' said Pritam gloomily. 'Now we have two pianos to get rid of.'

'Exactly,' said Melissa. 'And I know the perfect way of doing it.'

'We'll need more dynamite for two,' said Gaz.

Chapter Eighteen

On Saturday the church summer fête was to be held. Preparations began early and by the afternoon Rookhampton green was bustling with activity.

Melissa and Gaz sat on the pavement against Mrs Blake's wall, waiting.

Inside, Bella practised arpeggios.

'This is really boring,' said Gaz, scraping cement from between the bricks with a stone. 'We've been here for years. I don't know why Lee told us not to ring. What if she doesn't come out?'

'She's bound to,' said Melissa. 'Nobody misses the church fête. And we've only been here for twenty minutes according to *my* watch.'

'Do you think Mrs Blake is on to us?'

'Not her,' said Melissa. 'She's far too busy bossing people about in the refreshment tent.'

'I could be having a go on "Slosh the Vicar" instead of sitting here,' said Gaz. 'It's brilliant. You get wet sponges and . . .'

'It's pathetic,' said Melissa, 'and far too near to the bungalow. It's our job to keep Bella out of the way while they switch the pianos.'

The arpeggios stopped abruptly, and a few minutes later Bella opened the front door.

Gaz and Melissa were on the step.

'Hi,' said Melissa, holding the door open.

'You coming to the fête?' said Gaz.

'I have half an hour,' said Bella oddly.

She stared towards the green and blinked a little at its brightness.

'Is that all?' said Gaz.

'Let's go over to the tent,' said Melissa.

She took Bella's arm and led her to the gate, while Gaz wedged the front door open with his stone.

'I mustn't be long,' said Bella. 'I must practise.'

'Of course,' said Melissa, raising her eyes at Gaz. 'But you've got time for a Coke or something.'

'Yeah,' said Gaz enthusiastically. '*And* they've got doughnuts.'

They led Bella down the green towards the tent.

'There's a piano over there,' she said. 'Under one of the oak trees.'

'So there is,' said Gaz, grinning meaningfully at Melissa. 'I wonder why that's there.'

As soon as Gaz and Melissa had taken Bella into the refreshment tent, Pritam and Lee wheeled the Bechstein out of Florence's front garden.

'This thing weighs a ton,' said Pritam.

'It's massive,' said Lee. 'Thank goodness Miss Eisenhandler persuaded those guys off the green to get it downstairs. We'd never have managed it.'

They pushed it slowly along the road towards the bungalow.

'What if someone sees us?' said Pritam.

'Just act natural,' said Lee. 'They'll think it's something to do with the fête . . . which it is.'

Ten minutes later the Bechstein and the boys were standing in Mrs Blake's hall.

'I don't like this,' said Pritam anxiously. 'It's trespassing.'

'I know,' said Lee.

He opened Bella's door and peered in cautiously.

'It's got to go in here,' he whispered.

'Stop whispering,' whispered Pritam. 'You're making me nervous.'

Lee tiptoed over to Bella's window and opened it wide.

'What are you doing that for?' said Pritam.

'I'm just making sure it's not stuck,' said Lee.

'Are you crazy?' said Pritam. 'Mrs Blake might see you. For goodness' sake, let's get on with this.'

Fifteen minutes later, Pritam and Lee joined the others in the refreshment tent.

'Hi,' said Melissa crossly. 'We've just had to queue for ten minutes.'

'Yeah,' said Gaz. '*And* all the doughnuts had gone.'

Bella said nothing.

'Hello, Bella,' said Lee.

'Hello,' said Bella politely, without looking up. She took a sip from her can, though there was no Coke left.

'The conversation in here isn't up to much either,' said Melissa, pulling a face at Bella behind her back.

Lee noticed Florence in the tent entrance.

'Here's Miss Eisenhandler,' he said. 'Shall I ask her over, Bella?'

'That would be nice,' said Bella, without enthusiasm.

'I'll get her then,' said Lee.

Florence looked pale and her grey eyes were rimmed with red.

'Is everything all right?' she said anxiously.

'The pianos are in place,' said Lee. 'And Bella doesn't seem to suspect anything.'

'How is she?'

'Not good,' said Lee.

'She's getting up,' said Florence.

'Oh no,' said Lee. 'She can't go yet!'

But as Bella pushed past them, out on to the

green, a muffled announcement came over the loud speaker.

'*Ladies and Gentlemen, the piano-bashing competition is about to begin. The piano-bashing competition is about to begin.*'

Chapter Nineteen

Bella had only walked a short distance from the refreshment tent when she stopped, clutching her head as if in pain.

'It's the piano,' said Lee. 'I think she can hear it. Let's get her as far away from it as possible.'

'If she realizes what's going to happen, she'll stop the competition,' said Florence. 'We must get her off the green.'

They hurried after her.

'Bella, dear,' said Florence. 'You're just the person I want to see.'

'It needs me,' chanted Bella, staring into space. 'I must go to it.'

'Of course, dear,' said Florence, taking Bella's arm. 'Lee and I shall walk back to the bungalow with you.'

'I must practise,' said Bella.

Her eyes looked vacant.

'Let's get over there then,' said Lee, taking the other arm.

'*Please give a big cheer for our two teams,*' crackled the announcer, '*Rookhampton Youth Club and Little Barnfield Scouts, who have kindly agreed to this fund-raising contest at short notice.*'

Cheers.

Lee and Florence led Bella away.

Behind them, under separate oak trees, stood the two pianos. Beside each one, hanging from a branch like a noose, was an old car tyre.

Lee willed Bella not to look round.

'*Using an assortment of tools,*' said the announcer, '*each team must break their piano into pieces small enough to pass through a tyre. The team that is first to get the whole piano through their tyre will win the trophy, which has been donated by Mrs Pring, our Sunday School teacher.*'

More cheers.

Lee, Florence and Bella reached the bungalow door.

'Where's your key, dear?' said Florence.

Bella held her head.

'I hear you,' she said. 'You're not in there. I'm coming.'

Then she turned towards the two oak trees at the far end of the green.

'I hear you!' she cried.

She broke away from Lee and Florence and ran across the green towards the pianos.

'Stop her!' cried Florence.

Lee ran, but Bella was faster.

As she reached the edge of the crowd, a whistle blew and the competition began.

She pushed to the front and was about to scramble over the rope when an axe tore into the back of Bill Bartlett's piano. The panelling cracked sharply as it was wrenched away.

Bella hesitated.

Someone wrenched off the front panel and battered the interior with a sledgehammer. Strings twanged and snapped like ripping sinews. Torn wood, handfuls of keys and a pedal were passed through the tyre whilst a girl propped the piano lid against the tree trunk and crushed it with her boot.

Lee was beside Bella.

'Leave it, Bella,' he said. 'It's for the best.'

'Where are you?' she called. 'I can't hear you.'

But the piano was silent.

There was a roar of satisfaction as the Rookhampton Youth Club finished.

It was almost indecent.

A pathetic sprinkling of wood splinters lay where Bill Bartlett's piano had stood.

Bella turned to Lee, seeing him.

'Lee?' she said.

She felt strong again, alive, as if good blood had

been pumped back into her body. The piano was dead and Bella was free.

'Of course it's me, you dope,' said Lee, giving her a big hug.

Chapter Twenty

Lee was sitting by the knobbly oak tree, throwing and catching the squashy football, when Bella went out on Monday morning.

'Hi,' he said casually.

'Hi,' said Bella, pressing a stone into the grass with her shoe.

'I heard you practising,' said Lee. 'Didn't I?'

'Yes,' said Bella. 'It was me.'

'What do you make of Adelaide's piano then?'

'It's beautiful,' said Bella.

'And how's your gran?' he said, still throwing and catching.

'She's quite like my old granny again,' said Bella. 'And very proud to have a Bechstein in her bungalow. It makes her feel like royalty.'

'And Pawpaw?'

'He's back. He was scratching at the door when I got home this afternoon. He was starving, poor thing. He got out of the front door about a week ago and I hadn't seen him since.'

'I think that was my fault,' said Lee. 'He ran away when I did.'

'I think he'd have got out anyway,' said Bella. 'The way things were.'

'So everything's back to normal?' said Lee, throwing the ball as high as he could.

He still hadn't looked at her.

'Yes, silly,' said Bella. 'Scared I'm going to introduce you to some more ghosts, are you?'

She batted the ball out of his hands as he caught it and dribbled it away across the green.

'Give it back, Beetlebottom,' he shouted, pursuing her.

They kicked the football around for a few minutes before crashing down in a tangle of arms and legs.

'You're dangerous, you are,' said Lee, examining his knee. 'Look at this bruise.'

'It's a grass stain, Toadface,' said Bella. 'My internal injuries are far more serious.'

They heard a door slam.

'Bella!' called a voice.

'Look out,' said Lee, pretending to hide behind Bella. 'It's your gran . . . and she's got a weapon.'

'No she hasn't,' laughed Bella. 'It's a present for

Florence. We're going for lunch with her and Granny's bought her the biggest box of chocolates in the world.'

'Come on, dear,' called Mrs Blake, striding across the green. 'Sorry to interrupt your football, but we don't want to be late, do we?'

'I'll have to go,' said Bella.

She stood and brushed the grass off her clothes.

'I'll see you then,' said Lee. 'School starts tomorrow, but I'll still be at the Club.'

He held the football between his knees and butted it with his head.

'I'll look out for you,' said Bella. 'And, Lee . . .'

He looked up.

'Yes?'

'Thanks.'

He shrugged.

'That's OK,' he said.

Chapter Twenty-One

A week later, Bella returned to the bungalow from her first day at Bedeside Academy.

'How was it, dear?' said her granny, almost before Bella got through the door.

'Awful,' said Bella. 'The other girls all know each other and there aren't any spare friends left.'

'You'll soon get to know them. Things will be quite different in a week or so, you'll see.'

'*And* I got teased by the village kids because of my uniform. They have far more choice at the local school. It's not fair.'

'Doesn't anybody else from the village go to the Academy?'

'Only Melissa, but she doesn't have to go on the bus. It was really embarrassing.'

'How about the work? I'm sure you'll have no trouble with that.'

'It's fine,' admitted Bella. 'But you should see the amount of homework I've got. I shall be up all night, I expect.'

'You'll feel better when you've had some tea,' said her granny. 'Why not change into some of your nice new clothes while I get it ready. I've made your favourite chocolate cake.'

At eleven o'clock Bella was sitting on her bed with Pawpaw.

'Did you miss me today?' she said, stroking him under his chin.

He purred obligingly.

'They'd better not give me that amount of work every night,' she said. 'It's taken me ages.'

Pawpaw yawned hugely and stretched out his back paws.

'You're right,' said Bella. 'It's definitely bedtime. Granny went hours ago. I haven't touched the piano today, but it's far too late now.'

'Perhaps *I* can change your mind,' said the piano.

Its voice was resonant and percussive, with the cultured tone you would expect from a Bechstein. The menace in it made Bella stiffen.

Pawpaw tried to scrabble off the bed, but Bella held him tight.

'Might I suggest an hour's practice before you go to bed?' it said.

Bella knew she must ignore it.

'It's so quiet, Paws,' she said. 'I'll be asleep in no time.'

She yawned.

But Pawpaw kicked out of her arms, jumped down to the bedroom door and pulled at it with his paw.

'You *will* hear me,' said the Bechstein.

Bella stood slowly. Her limbs were like ice.

'OK,' she said. 'So I *can* hear you. But it doesn't mean I have to take any notice.'

'If you take no notice,' said the Bechstein evenly, 'you will have to be punished.'

Pawpaw clawed the door open and ran out.

'For what?' said Bella.

'For murder.'

Bella felt sick.

'I don't know what you're talking about,' she said.

'You seem to forget that your room overlooks the village green.'

'So?'

'You had that piano destroyed and I watched every minute of it. I admit that it was a common and nasty little instrument, but we pianos must stick together.'

The hairs on Bella's neck pricked her like pins.

'So do as I say, Bella Blake, or I may have to deal with you in the same way Mr Bartlett's piano dealt with him.'

Bella's eyes widened.

'I see you have heard of him. It was so easy to make it look like suicide, especially as he was not in his right mind at the time.'

'Pianos can't destroy people,' said Bella, edging her way towards the door.

'Try me,' it said. 'An hour's practice . . . or I shall show you how it is done.'

Chapter Twenty-Two

Bella escaped from the room, shut Pawpaw in the kitchen and hurried from the bungalow. She needed help, and there was only one person she could turn to.

It wasn't hard to find Oak Crescent. It curved round opposite Rookhampton allotments.

But the houses were all the same, and Bella had no idea which was Lee's.

She ran along the crescent, hoping desperately for a clue.

Some houses had lights on downstairs, some upstairs, but most were in darkness.

On one bedroom windowsill sat a lamp, with an ugly orange shade. There was something next to it. It looked like a pumpkin, gleaming in the light.

Bella had seen it before. She recognized the faded black markings. It was the squashy football from the green.

Someone came up to the window to close the curtains.

It was Lee. He pulled them half-shut then, as if he sensed that he was being watched, pressed his nose up against the window.

Bella waved her arms.

He stared for a second, then pulled the curtains tightly together.

It was too dark. He hadn't seen her. What should she do?

Bella turned, startled, as a cat yowled from the allotments. A piece of newspaper shuffled across the road towards her in the breeze. Bella shivered. She felt scared now. And cold. But there was no way she could face going back to that piano on her own.

'Hello,' whispered a voice behind her.

She turned.

It was Lee.

'It's you,' she said.

'I know *that*,' he said.

He sounded cross. She felt flustered and confused.

'You've got the communal football in your room,' she said.

'So? I kicked it down here with Gaz this evening, and neither of us could be bothered to take it back. We didn't think anybody would want it at this time of night. Surely you haven't come here to get that, have you?'

Bella shook her head. She felt like crying.

'You'll think I'm mad,' she said.

'I already do,' said Lee. 'So you may as well tell me.'

'It's all started again, Lee, and I'm so frightened.'

'What's started?'

'It's Adelaide's piano,' said Bella. 'It spoke to me. It says I've got to play it or it will deal with me . . . like the other piano did with Bartlett. You're the only one who can help me. I daren't let it get to Granny . . . I'm scared she might even be in with it now . . . and I can't tell Florence. She'd

be *so* upset. It's going to get me, Lee . . . What am I going to do?'

Lee put his arm around her and groaned.

'Before I met you, I thought pianos were things you played "Chopsticks" on,' he said.

'I *know* it sounds crazy,' said Bella. 'But it's true.'

Lee stared into her eyes and sighed. She was telling the truth all right.

'What can I do, Lee?' said Bella.

'You mean, what can *we* do,' said Lee.

'You'll come?'

He shrugged.

'Of course,' he said.

Chapter Twenty-Three

As they hurried back across the green, Bella and Lee could see that the bungalow was in darkness.

'That's odd,' said Bella. 'I'm sure I left my light on.'

'Perhaps your gran's woken up,' said Lee.

'I hope not,' said Bella grimly.

The front door was open a crack. They pushed it back and stepped into the dark hall.

Bella's door was open.

They stood very still, wondering what to do.

'Listen,' whispered Bella, grabbing hold of Lee's arm.

'What?' said Lee.

He felt like giggling. It was fear.

'I can hear Granny snoring,' whispered Bella.

'She must be all right then,' said Lee, trying to sound calm. He was reassured to feel a cool draught of air from the open front door behind them.

'We'll have to go in,' said Bella.

'Couldn't we reason with it from out here?' said Lee hopefully.

Bella put her hand round the door and clicked the light switch.

'Bulb's gone,' she said.

'We've got some spare ones at home,' said Lee. 'Want me to fetch one?'

But Bella pulled him into the room.

As they stepped inside they heard the dull thud of the front door closing.

'It's blown shut,' said Lee, putting his foot out to stop the bedroom door.

But they both knew it wasn't that windy.

'Never mind,' said Bella. 'It was getting a bit chilly anyway.'

Then the piano spoke.

'Step right inside,' it said. 'Both of you.'

The voice was evil. Menacing.

Lee felt his head jangling. He wanted to scream.

Bella let go of his arm and walked right into the room.

Lee tried to reach her without letting the door shut.

'Don't listen to it!' he said. 'Let's get out of here.'

He darted into the room and dragged her back

to the door. But it was already shut tight.

'*Now* you will listen,' said the piano.

'Leave us alone,' said Lee.

'Or else?' said the piano.

'Or else we'll bash you,' said Lee. 'Like we did with Bill Bartlett's piano.'

It laughed nastily, making Lee shiver.

'You seem to forget you are dealing with a Bechstein,' it said. 'Bechsteins do not "bash" easily.'

'You're just a lump of wood,' said Lee. 'You can't scare us.'

'Play me, Bella,' it said. 'Or I shall be forced to show him just what I *can* do.'

Bella walked towards it.

'Don't listen to it, Bella,' said Lee. 'It's getting to you.'

'Play me, Bella.'

'You'll be in its power if you do,' said Lee. 'Listen to *me*.'

He reached out to stop her, but he couldn't move.

'My legs, Bella,' he cried. 'It's my legs. I can't move them.'

'Just a little example of my powers,' said the Bechstein. 'Now perhaps you will stop interfering.'

Lee tried to shout for help, but he had no voice. All he could do was stand there in the dark, and listen.

'Play me, Bella,' said the Bechstein.

'I will,' chanted Bella. 'I will.'

But she didn't.

Suddenly, above the piano, appeared a broad shaft of silver light. And down it, like a fairy godmother, slid a small shimmering figure who landed rather clumsily on the stool, between Bella and the piano.

'Oh no you don't,' said the shiny lady, waggling a stern finger at the Bechstein. 'You needn't think you can misbehave yourself the moment my back is turned.'

Bella drew back to Lee, suddenly conscious again.

'I have been treated badly,' said the Bechstein.

Its voice was different now, almost sulky.

Lee's legs began to tingle as the feeling returned to them.

'What nonsense,' said the lady. 'Florence made an excellent choice in Bella. She has talent and she plays you well.'

'But not enough,' said the Bechstein.

Its voice was growing weaker.

'She's a child,' said Adelaide. 'She has her life to

live. And even if she *never* plays you as often as I did, you're just going to have to live with it. Do you understand?'

'Live with it . . .' echoed the Bernstein obediently.

'Good,' said the lady. 'I must leave now. But you can rest assured that I shall be watching you. Always.'

'Always,' said the Bechstein.

The lady slid jerkily up the shaft of light, fading to nothing as she went.

'You know who that was, don't you?' said Lee, blinking as the bedroom light came on.

'Adelaide Eisenhandler,' said Bella. 'And wasn't she brilliant for a beginner?'

THE END